THE THUNDERMAKER

written and illustrated by

ALAN SYLIBOY

NIMBUS
PUBLISHING LTD

Nimbus Publishing Limited
3731 Mackintosh St, Halifax, NS B3K 5A5
(902) 455-4286 nimbus.ca

NB1185

Printed and bound in Canada

Design: Jenn Embree

Library and Archives Canada Cataloguing in Publication

Syliboy, Alan, author
The thundermaker / Alan Syliboy.
Issued in print and electronic formats.

ISBN 978-1-77108-329-4 (bound).
—ISBN 978-1-77108-330-0 (pdf)

1. Micmac Indians—Juvenile fiction. I. Title.
PS8637.Y39T48 2015   jC813'.6   C2015-904292-5
C2015-904293-3

Nimbus Publishing acknowledges the financial support for its publishing activities from the Government of Canada through the Canada Book Fund (CBF) and the Canada Council for the Arts, and from the Province of Nova Scotia. We are pleased to work in partnership with the Province of Nova Scotia to develop and promote our creative industries for the benefit of all Nova Scotians.

There is smoke coming from the top of a wigwam deep in the forest.

The trees are swaying a little, back and forth. The wind rises.
A summer storm must be coming.

Distant thunder is rumbling. The thunder gets louder. And louder.
The wind grows stronger. And stronger.

Then the ground starts to shake.

Inside the wigwam, a mother is talking to her son.

Her name is Giju, and she comes from a long line of storytellers. Her voice is soft and comforting. She is telling her boy a story about the thunder.

"You are from a long line of thundermakers," she tells him. "Your father is Big Thunder, and it is he who makes the thunder. You are Little Thunder, and one day you will bring the thunder to the world."

Big Thunder joins his family at the fire.

Little Thunder has many questions. "Where does the thunder come from?" he asks.

"It comes from within the earth," says Big Thunder, "and it helps to create new life. It is my job to gather up the thunder and lightning and throw it back to Earth carefully so it doesn't do damage or get trapped in one place."

"Can it hurt us?" asks Little Thunder.

"Well," Giju says, "lightning can start a fire and scorch the earth, but it also burns down the old trees and makes room for the new ones. Life sprouts from the earth's scar and that helps everything in the forest: the trees and plants and animals. This is called renewal, and it is part of the great circle of life."

Outside, the thunder dies down. The storm begins to move on. Little Thunder thinks about how much fun it will be to take his father's place as the Thundermaker, throwing lightning bolts and making the ground shake.

As the days pass, Little Thunder learns many other things.

From Giju, he learns that when he hears peepers in the spring, it means the fish are moving up the river.

His mother also shows him how to make the weirs that capture the fish. Together they build them out of stones that form a V in the shallow part of the river.

Once the fish are trapped, Little Thunder and Giju wade into the river, gather up the fish, and put them in the baskets they have made from reeds and moss.

Then the caribou and moose and deer arrive. Little Thunder learns from his father that the fish, the caribou, the moose, and the deer are all part of the same great circle of life. "And we are part of that great circle, too," Big Thunder tells him.

As the days get longer and warmer, Little Thunder picks the berries that grow in the forest.

When the days are finished, he spends the nights dreaming about making big thunder.

Soon winter comes. It is Little Thunder's favourite time to spend with his mother, for she tells him stories every night.

Little Thunder learns about story cycles. Giju explains how one cycle rolls into the next. She says that characters always reappear with a new teaching or a new way of telling an old one.

His mother talks in pictures, and these pictures transport him back in time. There, he can find his place as a part of this cycle.

When Little Thunder's mother finishes a story, his father picks it up, telling of great hunting trips and how to think like a rabbit or a fox. He tells Little Thunder how to know where the animals will be and how to have real respect for these creatures.

As Little Thunder gets older, his father gives him lessons on how to become the Thundermaker. His task is an important one for the Mi'kmaw people: he must create Kluskap, the teacher, by throwing three thunderbolts at a mound of clay.

Little Thunder has to pay close attention to how he throws the bolts and where they go.

"Throwing lightning bolts can be very dangerous," Big Thunder tells him. "There are consequences for any mistakes."

Little Thunder is a good student, and one day the time finally comes. He is ready to go to the sacred mountain and become the Thundermaker.

Little Thunder must complete his task alone,
but his lifelong friend, Wolverine, is curious.

Wolverine sneaks up the mountain,
following Little Thunder.

When Little Thunder turns around,
Wolverine changes into a tree.

Little Thunder keeps going, but is sure he is being followed.
He stops again and turns around quickly.

Wolverine hides behind a boulder, but Little Thunder sees him.
"Wolverine, I know that's you," he says. "Since you're here
already, you might as well come along."

At the top of the sacred mountain, Little Thunder
builds a fire and sings the song his father taught him.
He asks the Creator to help him become the Thundermaker.

Kisu'lk apoqinmu'i, Ke apoqinmu'i Kisu'lk.

In the language of his people, it means,
"Creator, help me. Please help me, Creator."

As soon as Little Thunder finishes the song,
the fire becomes a portal to the Spirit World.

Little Thunder knows that three thunderbolts are needed to create Kluscap, the teacher. But just as he prepares to throw his first thunderbolt through the portal, Wolverine whispers in Little Thunder's ear.

Little Thunder is distracted and throws the thunderbolt into the middle of a river, killing the fish.

Immediately, the ceremonial guardian, Hurricane Man, appears and scolds Little Thunder and Wolverine.

"Take more care in your task," he says sternly.

Little Thunder throws his second thunderbolt, and his aim is true. He hits a mound of clay, which immediately turns into a human figure.

He begins to throw his next thunderbolt but is again distracted by Wolverine whispering in his ear...

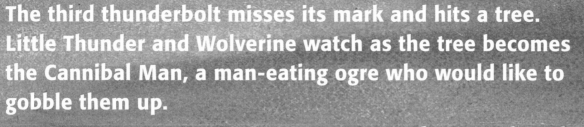

The third thunderbolt misses its mark and hits a tree. Little Thunder and Wolverine watch as the tree becomes the Cannibal Man, a man-eating ogre who would like to gobble them up.

Just then, Earthquake Man, a terrifying chief and Cannibal Man's mortal enemy, appears and stomps the ground.

He continues to stomp the ground until he creates an earthquake that swallows up the Cannibal Man.

Earthquake Man stomps again, knocking Little Thunder and Wolverine to the ground.

"I was here to help you this time," he scolds, "but you must take better care."

Little Thunder must land a second thunderbolt. He is nervous, but does not listen to Wolverine this time. He concentrates on his task, like his father taught him, and throws the thunderbolt…

The thunderbolt hits its mark, and the human form of clay is given life.

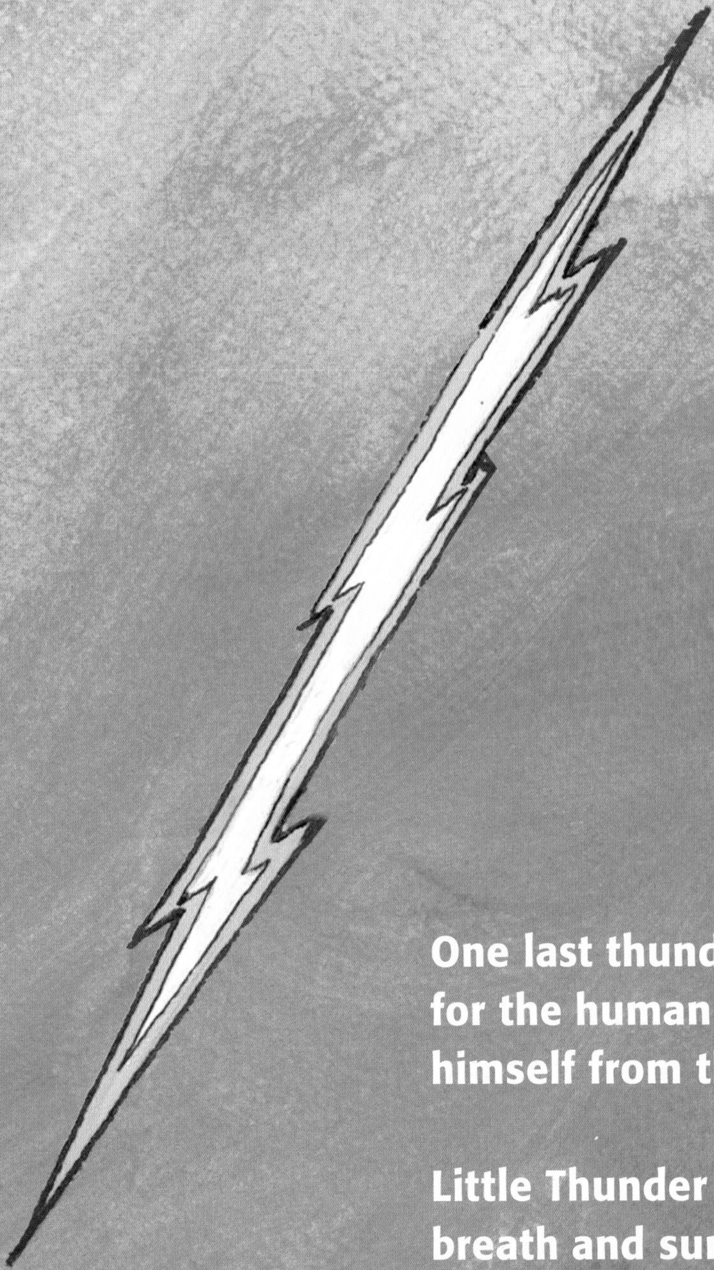

One last thunderbolt is needed
for the human being to free
himself from the land.

Little Thunder takes a deep
breath and summons a final
thunderbolt—and throws it…

The bolt lands. The human form becomes Kluscap the teacher, and he is freed from the earth.

Kluskap gathers medicines from the forest and then journeys to the village to meet his people, who he will teach and care for.

From the mountaintop, looking back through the portal,
Big Thunder and Wolverine are very pleased.

Little Thunder has accomplished an important task by
creating Kluscap, who is a great benefit to the Mi'kmaw people.

As a reward, he finally becomes…